To Rizzo, Hoban, Quincy, Coco, Cole, and George,
The best of pets and friends.

Rizzo was a normal dog,
except for just one quirk.

Rizzo had a silly tongue that simply would not work.

Up and down, left and right,
he simply couldn't stop.
He licked faces.

He licked hands.

He even licked a rock.

Rizzo's brothers tried to teach him to keep it in his mouth,

but controlling his tongue he simply couldn't figure out.

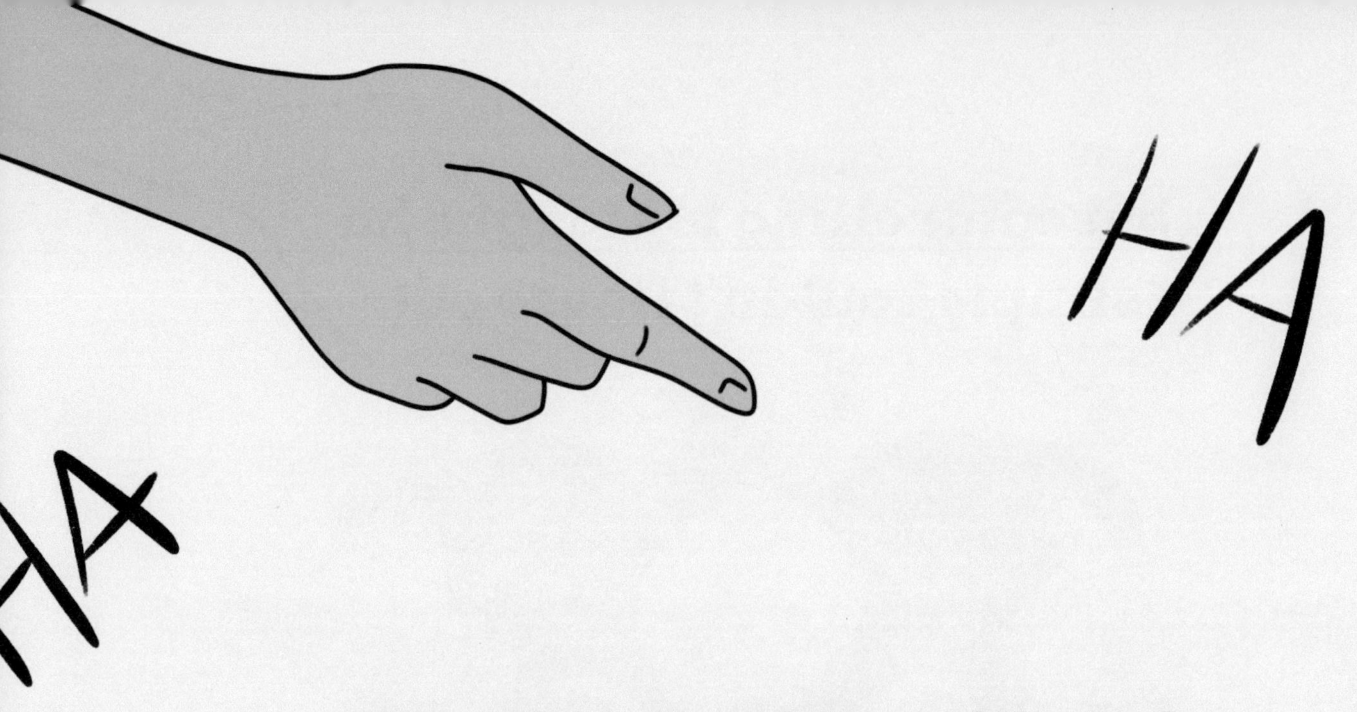

People called him odd, and that really hurt his heart,

so Rizzo's parents showed him something to give him a brand new start.

First, they showed him lizards,
geckos, chameleons all alike

With silly tongues just like him, they used them to catch flies!

Second, they showed him giraffes,
with necks a mile high

With slobbery tongues to match, used to eat leaves up near the sky.

Then they showed him frogs.
Those he liked the most.

Rizzo liked their cheeks and hops,
and mostly how they croaked!

His parents told him,
"Rizzo, you've been perfect all
along."

Rizzo thought, maybe just maybe,
he wasn't made wrong.

"You're just a little toad," they said,
"Dressed up as a dog."

From then on he was know fondly by all as Rizzo...

Rizzo the Furry Frog

The End

Rizzo's Brothers

The Real Hoban

The Real Quincy

The Real Rizzo

Made in the USA
Columbia, SC
20 January 2025